MW00876956

This book belongs to

Austin

With hugs and kisses to my three little Pandas,
Ilyse, Ilijah, and Ian.
—T.J.M.
With love to my Aunt Debbie.
—A.B.

Library of Congress Cataloging-in-Publication Data is available.

2 4 6 8 10 9 7 5 3 1

Published by Sterling Publishing Co., Inc. 387 Park Avenue South, New York, NY 10016

Text copyright © 2007 by Tara Jaye Morrow
Illustrations © 2007 by Aaron Boyd

Designed and produced for Sterling by COLOR-BRIDGE BOOKS, LLC, Brooklyn, NY

Distributed in Canada by Sterling Publishing
c/o Canadian Manda Group, 165 Dufferin Street
Toronto, Ontario, Canada M6K 3H6
Distributed in the United Kingdom by GMC Distribution Services
Castle Place, 166 High Street, Lewes, East Sussex, England BN7 1XU
Distributed in Australia by Capricorn Link (Australia) Pty. Ltd.
P.O. Box 704, Windsor, NSW 2756, Australia

Printed in China
All rights reserved

Sterling ISBN-13: 978-1-4027-4313-9 ISBN-10: 1-4027-4313-0

For information about custom editions, special sales, premium and corporate purchases, please contact
Sterling Special Sales Department at 800-805-5489 or specialsales@sterlingpub.com.

Panda Goes to School

By Tara Jaye Morrow • Illustrated by Aaron Boyd

STERLING

New York / London

"Good morning, Panda," whispered Mama.

Panda took the covers from his face and rubbed his eyes. "What day is it?" he asked.

"Don't you remember?" Mama replied. "Today is the first day of school."

"I don't think I can go today," said Panda.

"Why not?" Mama asked.

"Because we always eat breakfast together," Panda said. "I don't think you should eat all by yourself."

Mama smiled. "Don't worry, Panda," she said. "We are going to eat breakfast together. As soon as you get dressed."

Panda stopped a minute to think. "But who will help you water your plants if I'm not here? You shouldn't have to water your plants all by yourself, Mama."

"We can do it together, Panda. I've already filled the watering can. All we have to do now is pour."

"What about lunch?" Panda asked at breakfast.
"I usually help make the sandwiches, remember?
You will be very hungry if I go to school today."

"How about we make our sandwiches right now, before you go to school?" suggested Mama. "That way I won't be hungry while you're away."

After breakfast, Panda helped Mama pack his new backpack.
"And don't worry about playtime, either, Panda," Mama said.
"We'll play together when you get home at three."

But Panda felt very worried. And he was a little frustrated, too. Didn't Mama understand how hard this day would be for her without him around?

Mama helped Panda into his jacket and handed him his backpack.

Together, they walked to Panda's school. Then Panda
kissed his mama good-bye at the door.

Panda walked into his classroom. He saw lots
of other children, and he met his teacher.
"Welcome to school, Panda!" Teacher said.
Panda was trying really hard not to cry.

Teacher showed Panda where to hang his jacket and put away his backpack in the cubby with his name on it.

Then it was time for the children to get to know one another. When Teacher asked everyone's favorite foods, Panda said to himself, *Mama's pancakes.*

When it was time to tell their favorite song, Panda thought, *Any song my mama sings.*

When Teacher asked Panda's favorite thing to do,
Panda whispered, "I like playing with my mama."

Suddenly Panda jumped up from the table, ran to his cubby, and buried his nose in his jacket. Then he wailed, "I MISS MY MAMA!"

Some of the children were quite surprised, and a few began to sniffle, too.

But Teacher knew just what to do. She put
her arm around Panda's shoulder and asked if
he thought now was a good time for lunch.

"Yes," said Panda shyly.
"Good," said Teacher to Panda
and his classmates, "because today
we're having a picnic!"

All the children hurried to get their lunch boxes from their cubbies. Then they gathered around their teacher in a circle on the floor.

Panda sat down and opened his lunch box. There he found the cucumber sandwich he and Mama had made together, the box of juice they had packed together, and the apple slices Mama had cut and Panda had wrapped up that morning.

But Panda also found something else.

At the very bottom was a picture of Panda and Mama with a little note that said . . .

I am very proud of you, Panda.
You are a big boy.
Have a great day at school!

Panda smiled a very big smile. He showed the picture to his classmates. Then he put it in his pocket.

He felt happy for the rest of the day because he had his mama with him, after all. And he had a lot of fun at school that afternoon.

At three o'clock, Mama met Panda outside.
He ran up to her and gave her a tight squeeze.
"How was your day, Panda?" she asked.

"It was great, Mama! I met new friends, and we had a picnic, and played games, and you know the best part?"

"What's that?" she asked.

Panda pulled the picture from his pocket. "The best part is that you were at school with me," he said.

When Panda got home, he sat right down to draw a picture of himself and his mama. Then he asked Mama to write down a little poem that he made up while he was drawing.

It said . . .

When I'm at school and Mama's home,
I'm having fun.
I'm not alone.

Here's a picture of you and me.
Keep it in your pocket.
I'll be home at three.

Happy School Days!
Love, Panda